D1372117

Evan's Corner

Evan's Corner

by Elizabeth Starr Hill

illustrated by Nancy Grossman

Holt, Rinehart and Winston   New York   Chicago   San Francisco

To my godson,
Wilson MacDonald,
with love
from Aunt Betty.

Evan walked
home from school slowly.
He stopped in front of a pet shop.

In the window, a canary
sang to him from its golden
cage.

Canary bird has its own
cage, Evan thought. *I want a
place of my own.*

He walked on. A bright pink
flower on a window sill caught
his eye. Flower has its own pot,
he thought. Wish *I* had a place
of my own.

He kept going until he reached the big crossing. He waited by the newsstand for the light to change.

Paper man has his own stand, he thought. And I, me, myself—*I* need a place of my own.

He crossed the noisy, busy street and turned into the building where he lived. He trudged up four flights of steep stairs to the two rooms that he and his family shared.

Soon his three sisters and his two brothers would come home. Then his mother and then his father.

Mighty lot of family, Evan thought. And no place to call just *mine*.

Evan wore a door key on a string around his neck so he could unlock the door. Usually he was the first one home. But today the door flew open before he touched it.

"Surprise!" His mother stood laughing in the doorway. "Mrs. Thompson said I could leave early. I beat you home, Evan!" Mrs. Thompson was the lady his mother cleaned for.

Evan gave his mother a big hug. He liked it when she got home ahead of him. Now they could have a private talk before his brothers and sisters came in.

"Mamma, you know what I've been wishing for *hard?*" Evan burst out.

"Tell me." His mother smiled.

Evan told her the canary bird had a cage. He told her the flower had a pot. He told her the paper man had a newsstand. He ended, "And *I* want a place of my own."

His mother thought and thought. At first it seemed she might not find a way.

But then her face lighted up. "Why, of course!" she said. "It will work out just right. There are eight of us. That means each one of us can have a corner!"

Evan jumped to his feet and clapped his hands. "Can I choose mine?"

"Yes." She nodded. "Go ahead. You have first choice, Evan."

Evan ran to every corner of the rooms. One corner had a pretty edge of rug. Some had nothing much. One had an interesting crack in the wall.

But the one Evan liked best, the one he wanted for his own, had a nice small window and a bit of polished floor.

"This is mine," Evan said happily. "This is my corner."

Evan's mother had no kitchen. She shared the kitchen down the hall with another lady. Often Evan went with her to keep her company while she fixed supper.

But that night he paid no attention to the rest of the family. He sat alone and content on the floor, in his corner.

His little brother Adam asked him, "Why you want a corner of your own, Evan?"

Evan thought for a minute. "I want a chance to be lonely."

Adam tiptoed away and left him.

When supper was ready, Evan's father came to Evan's corner.

"Stew's on the table," he told him. "You want to eat with us, Evan?"

"Please, Pa," Evan asked, "if I bring my plate here, can I eat by myself?"

"Why, sure," his father said.

So Evan fetched his plate of stew and sat down on the floor again.

His family ate at the table in the next room. From his corner, Evan could see them. He heard them talking and laughing.

At dessert time, he joined them.

"Why, Evan!" His father smiled. "I thought you wanted to eat by yourself."

Evan smiled back at him. "I was lonely," he said.

After supper, there were jobs to do. Evan helped clear the table. He brushed his teeth. He studied for school.

When his work was done, he sat in his corner again. He looked out the window.

The sky was almost dark. Two pigeons cooed sleepily on the window ledge. Stars lighted up, one by one. The breeze blew cooler.

Adam came behind Evan and said softly, "Are you being lonely now?"

"No," Evan answered.

"What *are* you doing then?"

"I'm wasting time," Evan told him. "In my own way. In my own corner."

Adam asked, "Can I ever come into your corner, Evan?"

"Why don't you choose a corner of your own?" Evan said.

So Adam did. He chose the corner across the room from Evan's. He sat in it. He called, "What shall I do in my corner, Evan?"

"Whatever you like."

But Adam didn't know what to do. After a minute, he left his corner. He played horse with his big sister Lucy. He sat on her back and held on to her pigtails. "Gid-yup, Lucy-horse!" he shouted. They galloped round and round the room.

Evan watched the pigeons fall asleep on the ledge. He watched the sky get darker and the stars get brighter.

Finally his father called him, "Come out of your corner, sleepyhead! It's time for bed!"

Next morning, as soon as he woke up, Evan ran to his corner. His bit of polished floor shone as brightly as ever. His window was still fun to look through.

But Evan felt that his corner needed something more. What could it be?

He stared at the bare walls. I know! he thought suddenly. I need me a picture! And I'll make it myself!

In school that morning, Evan painted a picture of the sea. He drew big waves and a green boat.

He told his teacher, "I'm going to hang this picture in my own corner!"

"That will be lovely, Evan," his teacher said.

Evan could hardly wait to get home after school. He ran past the pet shop.

"Canary bird!" he shouted over his shoulder. "I got a place of my own now! I'm going to hang a picture in it!"

A-skip and a-gallop, he passed the window sill with the flower pot.

"Listen, old pink flower," he told it, "I got a place of my own! And I made me a picture for it!"

He skidded to a stop at the corner. He waited for the light to change. He spoke to the man at the newsstand. "Guess what, mister!"

"What, little boy?"

"I'm going to hang this picture in a place that's *just mine!*"

And he skipped and rushed and almost flew the rest of the way.

He taped the picture to the wall beside the window in his corner. He stepped back to look at it.

The green boat seemed to bob on the blue waves. It bobbed too much. Evan realized the picture was crooked.

He straightened it. Now it looked just right.

Adam came home with their biggest sister, Gloria. She always picked Adam up at the day-care center on her way home from school.

Adam's eyes shone as he saw the picture. "That's mighty pretty, Evan!" he said. "Do you think I could draw a picture for my corner?"

"Sure you could."

Adam ran off. But he could not find any paper. He had no crayons. Lucy had, but she was busy with homework now. He did not dare speak to her.

He returned to Evan.

Evan sat in his corner with his back to the room. He looked up at his picture.

Adam asked softly, "Are you being lonely, Evan?"

"No."

"Are you wasting your own time in your own way?"

"No," Evan told him.

"Well, then, what are you doing?"

"Enjoying peace and quiet," Evan said.

Adam tiptoed off.

That night, Evan did not sleep well. He lay awake in bed, thinking about his corner.

It had a nice floor and a nice window and a nice picture. But was that enough?

No, he decided finally. I need something more.

But what?

He remembered the pink flower in its pot. He thought:
That's it! I need a plant of my own, in my own corner.

On Saturday, Evan went to the playground. He took his toothbrush glass and a spoon.

The paving of the playground was cracked. Grass and weeds grew up through the broken concrete.

Evan found a weed that had big, lacy flowers on it. He dug it up with his spoon. He planted it in his toothbrush glass.

Then he took it home and put it on the window sill, in his own corner.

Adam came over to see what was going on. "What you doing, Evan?" he asked.

"Watching my plant grow," Evan told him.

"Maybe I'll have a plant, too, someday," Adam said softly.

Evan didn't answer. Something was bothering him.

Even now, his corner seemed not quite perfect. And he didn't know why.

I got me no furniture, he realized at last. Why didn't I think of that before?

Evan skipped off to the grocery store. He asked Mr. Meehan for two old orange crates.

"What do you want them for?" Mr. Meehan asked.

"Going to make me some furniture," Evan said proudly. "To put in a place of my own."

Mr. Meehan let him have the crates.

In his corner, Evan stood one of the crates up on end.
Now it was like a high desk. He turned the other crate
upside down to make a bench. He sat on the bench.
Surely he had all anyone could wish for.

And yet…

How come I feel like something's still missing? Evan
wondered.

He puzzled and puzzled it over. Suddenly he remembered the canary bird in its cage.

A great idea struck him: I know! I need a pet to take
care of. A pet of my own, in my own corner.

And he ran out to the pet shop.

He looked at the canary bird in the window. Well, canary bird, he thought, you sing fine. But you're not the pet for me.

He walked into the store. A goldfish swam over to the edge of its bowl and stared at him.

"Afternoon, Mister Fish," Evan said politely. But he thought: No sir. That's not the pet for me.

He moved on to the turtle tank. A sign above it read: "Bargain! Special! Turtle with bowl, only 50c!" Beside the tank, a neat row of empty little bowls waited.

Evan peered into the tank. Ten or twelve lively baby green turtles swam and scrambled all over each other.

One climbed up on a rock in the middle of the water. It looked at Evan. He felt like laughing. It must have been the funniest turtle in the world!

That baby turtle had the *scrawniest* neck. Its feet were big and ugly. Its eyes were merry and black. If a turtle could smile, that turtle was smiling.

It took a dive off the rock. Clumsy turtle! It landed upside down in the shallow water! Its legs waved wildly in the air.

Evan turned it over carefully. The turtle winked at him as though it knew a secret. It looked as cheerful as ever.

"Yes sir, yes sir!" Evan told that funny little turtle joyfully. "*You're* the pet for me!"

Evan's heart beat hard and fast. He asked the pet-shop man, "Please, mister, do you have a job a boy can do? I'd mighty much like to earn enough to buy a turtle!"

"Sorry, son, I don't need help. Try next door," the pet-shop man suggested.

Evan went next door to the Chinese bakery and asked for work. "Ah, no," Mr. Fong told him gently. "My sons help me. Try across the street."

Evan crossed the street. He marched from store to store, asking for work. He had no luck.

Maybe some lady would pay me to carry her packages, Evan thought.

He turned in at the supermarket. He stood by the check-out counter. A lady came through. Evan asked, "Carry your bags, lady?"

She did not answer. She walked on by.

Evan waited for the next lady. This time he smiled extra

politely and spoke a little louder. "Excuse me, but those bags look mighty heavy. Carry them for you?"

"Why, yes." She put them in his arms. "That would be a big help."

Evan carried the groceries up the block to where she lived. The lady thanked him. She gave him a dime.

A dime! He had a dime! Now all he needed was four more!

Evan raced back to the supermarket. He stood by the check-out. He waited. He smiled. He spoke politely.

Lots of ladies went past. But none of them wanted him to carry her bags.

Just as Evan began to fear that he would never make another cent, a young girl said, "Oh, good! I hate lugging bundles!"

She, too, gave Evan a dime.

Only three more to go, he thought happily.

On Sunday the supermarket was closed. But Evan went there right after school on Monday.

He made one more dime, then another. He had forty cents!

Listen, you turtle! he thought. You're almost mine!

But the next day, he fooled around for a while after school. When he finally got to the supermarket, a bigger boy was there ahead of him.

Evan's heart sank. He had supposed it would be so easy to earn only one dime! He hung around all afternoon, hoping. But the other boy got the jobs. And Evan still had only forty cents.

Next day he rushed from school to the supermarket as fast as his legs would go. Panting, he ran right to the check-out counter. The other boy was not there!

Hurray! Evan thought. Bet this is my lucky day!

At first things were slow. Then, toward closing time, a marvelous moment came. A white-haired lady spoke to him: "Sonny, do you think you could help me with these heavy groceries?"

Evan said eagerly, "Yes *ma'am!*"

Her bag was still on the counter. It was a huge one, filled clear up to the top. Somehow Evan got his arms around it and hoisted it off the counter. "Where to, lady?" he gasped.

"Why," she said sweetly, "I live just next door." She added, "Three flights up."

Evan staggered out of the store with the bag. He followed the lady next door without much trouble. But he

thought he never *would* get up those stairs.

Yet at last he made it. He eased the bag down on the lady's kitchen table.

"Thank you," she said. And she gave him the dime— the wonderful dime—the shining dime that made five!

Evan ran to the pet shop at top speed. He poured the dimes on the counter and said proudly, "I earned some money, mister! I'd like to buy me a turtle!"

The pet-shop man counted the dimes. "All right, son. Choose one," he said.

Evan looked into the tank. His eyes passed from one shining green shell to another.

Suddenly he saw a scrawny neck stretch up from the water. A turtle rose, climbed the rock—and fell off upside down, on his back.

"This one!" Evan picked the turtle up. "This one is mine!"

Evan carried the turtle home in a small bowl. He set it on top of the upturned orange crate.

Adam was already home from the day-care center. He asked excitedly, "What you got now, Evan?"

"My own pet," Evan boasted. "To take care of, in my own corner."

Adam looked at the turtle. It winked at him cheerfully.

Adam wanted to see it closer. But he knew he wasn't allowed in Evan's corner.

"Evan, do you think I could ever have a pet of my own?" Adam asked.

"Sure. When you're much, much older."

Adam wandered sadly away.

Now Evan had many things.

He had a place of his own. He could be lonely there. He could waste time if he liked. He could enjoy peace and quiet.

He had a fine picture to look at.

He had a bench of his own to sit on, by his own window. His plant thrived and grew tall.

Best of all, he had a pet to love and take care of.

Evan spent most of his spare time in his corner. But— it was strange. He just wasn't happy.

I must need something more, Evan thought. But what?

He asked his sisters. They didn't know.

He asked his brothers. They didn't know.

His father wasn't home yet. When his mother came home, Evan said, "Mama, I'm not happy in my corner. What do I need now?"

His mother put her head on one side. Together she and Evan stood off from the corner and looked at it.

Sunlight poured through the window and gleamed on the floor.

The lacy white flower stirred in a breeze.

The turtle seemed to grin through the glass of its bowl.

The painted boat rode a painted wave.

Evan's corner was beautiful. They both saw that.

"Evan," his mother said finally. "Maybe what you need is to leave your corner for a while."

"Why?" Evan asked.

"Well," she said slowly, "just fixing up your own corner isn't enough." She smiled into his eyes. "Maybe you need to step out now, and help somebody else."

She left him. He sat alone on his bench, thinking it over.

Adam came in. "Are you enjoying peace and quiet, Evan?" he asked.

"No," Evan said.

"What *are* you doing, then?"

Evan said slowly, "I'm planning to borrow Lucy's crayons."

"Why?"

"To help you draw a picture if you want to. I'm planning to help you fix up your corner so it's just the way you want it. I'm going to help you make it the best—

the nicest—

the very most wonderful corner in the whole world!"

Joy spread over Adam's face—and over Evan's.

They ran across the room together to work on Adam's corner.